The Reactor

Jillian Powell

Illustrated by
Paul Savage

Titles in Full Flight

Badger Publishing Limited
26 Wedgwood Way, Pin Green Industrial Estate, Stevenage, Hertfordshire SG1 4QF
Telephone: 01438 356907. Fax: 01438 747015.
www.badger-publishing.co.uk   enquiries@badger-publishing.co.uk

The Reactor   ISBN 1 85880 924 X

Series Editor: Jonny Zucker.
Publisher: David Jamieson.
Editor: Paul Martin.
Cover design: Jain Birchenough.
Cover illustration: Paul Savage.
Printed and bound in China through Colorcraft Ltd., Hong Kong

The Reactor

Jillian Powell

Illustrated by
Paul Savage

Contents

Badger Publishing

Chapter 1 - The Staircase

"Me first." The others stood aside.

"Count how many seconds to the bottom," Joe said.

The staircase curled below like an iron snake.

"Here goes!" Joe let out a battle cry.

Then he pushed off, sliding faster and faster, round and round.

"Five seconds!" Roy shouted.

The others followed, one after the other. They landed in a heap at the bottom.

"Wicked!" Joe said.

"Cool," Asif nodded.

There was always something new to do in the Reactor. That was their name for it.

It was just an old building really. But people once said they had carried out nuclear experiments there.
Joe came up with the name and it stuck. It was a great place.

- It had blank walls where the gang could spray graffiti.
- It had long corridors they could skateboard along.
- It had dark, empty cupboards where they could hide things.

The hardest part was getting in. But the gang had mastered that. They knew all the secret entrances.

Chapter 2 - Keep Out

"That's weird."

Joe and his mates were on their way to the Reactor.

"There's a sign on the gate," Joe said.

"What does it say?"

"Keep Out." Joe read aloud.

"Look! There's wire on top of the walls," Roy pointed out. "And the gates are locked."

Joe scrambled up on the gate.

"There's a geezer inside with a dog," he said. "He looks nasty."

"The geezer or the dog?

"Both."

They hung around, wondering what to do.

"It's not fair," Doug said. "The Reactor is our place."

Just then the dog started barking inside the yard.

"Let's go round the back," Joe said.

"Try the other entrance".

It said 'Keep Out' there too.

They could hear someone in the yard, with a dog on a chain.

"That's it, then," Roy said. "What do we do now?"

"Wait." Joe was thinking.

"The bunker!"

The bunker was an old coalbunker. Its entrance was a manhole in the ground. It was covered in grass and leaves.

And it was outside the fence.

Chapter 3 - The Bunker

It was dark inside the bunker. It smelt of coal and stale air.

Joe felt for the ladder that led into the Reactor.

"There it is!" Asif said.

"Shush!"

They scrambled up the ladder one after the other. They were inside a corridor that led to the labs.

"Smells like a hospital," Roy said, holding his nose.

They could hear voices coming from one of the labs.

They crept silently along the corridor closer to the voices.

"Listen!"

"She is ageing faster than expected," a female voice said.

"We need to keep an eye on her."

Asif pulled a face.

"Who are they talking about?" he whispered.

"Must be a patient," Roy said. "It's a hospital, I reckon. Look."

He had pushed one of the lab doors ajar. Inside, they could see rows of glass jars and trays marked with labels.

"Specimens," Roy said.

"Specimens of what?"

"Shush!" Joe said. The voices had gone quiet. The meeting was ending.

Joe pushed the others inside the open door. People were walking back to their labs. They wore white coats, like doctors.

Just then, Roy's watch began beeping. The footsteps outside slowed down.

"Did you hear something?" a voice said.

Joe pushed the others inside one of the cupboards.

They heard the lab door creak open. Somebody said something about a digital timer going off. Then the door was closed behind them.

"Phew, that was close," Joe whispered.

But Roy and the others were speechless. Roy nodded to Joe at the shelf behind them.

In the dark, he could hardly make out what it was. But it looked like a tray of human ears.

Chapter 4 - Penned Up

"Joe!"

Mr Young's voice boomed across the classroom.

"This is a maths lesson, not an art lesson."

He held up Joe's picture of an ear.

Everyone laughed, except for the gang. They had been thinking about the ears too.

By morning break, Asif had come up with a theory.

"It must be a lab where they study dead bodies and what they died from," he suggested.

"My cousin is a doctor. He had to do dead bodies at college. He had to cut up faces and stuff."

"But they were talking about someone ageing," Roy reminded them. "They can't all be dead people in there."

"There's only one way to find out," Joe said. "We will have to go back in tonight."

The bunker lid came up easily this time. They were soon inside, creeping along the corridors.

"We could try the basement," Asif whispered. "They have to keep the dead bodies somewhere."

Roy pulled a face.

"Why don't we just look in the lab with the trays and stuff?" he said.

But Joe was already sliding down the stair rail, into the basement.

The others were about to follow when they heard a rumbling noise.

Joe hid as a giant trolley rumbled towards him.

Then he signalled that the way was clear.

"It said clinical waste on the side," he told the others. "Roy must be right. It's some sort of hospital."

"Clinical waste could be..." Asif fell silent. They could hear a strange noise. It sounded like... but it couldn't be.

Joe led the others along the corridor and stopped by a door. He slipped inside.

There was a sweet smell of warm hay. Something pushed against Joe's leg. He put his hand out and felt in the dark. His fingers sank into thick wool.

They were inside a pen of sheep.

Chapter 5 - The Freezer

"Anybody got a torch?"

Roy felt in his pocket. "Here."

Joe shone the torch round the pen. There must be fifty or sixty sheep there. Joe swung the torch around. The pool of light shone on faces, legs, tails.

"They are all the same," he whispered.

"Sheep usually are," Roy said flatly. "That's why you count them when you are trying to sleep."

"No, look." Joe shone the torch for the others.

The sheep were all exactly the same size and colour.

They had black markings on their faces and legs, in exactly the same places.

"They are clones," Joe said slowly. "I'm sure of it. They are identical."

"I've just trodden in something," Roy said. "Can we get out of here?"

"OK, we'll take another look at the lab upstairs," Joe agreed. "Those trays had labels."

But the labels were not much help.

They were just a jumble of letters and numbers.

"What's this?" Doug had found a freezer. He opened the lid and some cold white smoke escaped.

"You don't think there are frozen heads in there, do you?" Roy said.

"They don't do head transplants, stupid," Joe said. "Mind you, it wouldn't be a bad idea for Roy."

"No," Roy said. "But some people have their heads frozen. So they can be brought back to life in the future. I read about it."

"They're not heads," Joe said. "But they might be eggs. They keep them frozen. For making babies."

Just then, they heard a dog barking. It was time to get out.

Chapter 6 - Remember Dolly?

"Read this stuff on cloning," Joe said. The gang were on the internet at Joe's house.

"Yeah, but they've done that," Asif said. "Don't you remember Dolly the Sheep? Why should it be so hush-hush if that's all they're doing?"

Joe shook his head. "That's what we're going to find out."

He was climbing up the ladder from the bunker, when he heard footsteps.

A woman in a white coat walked past. She slid open a window and checked inside one of the rooms.

She wrote something down on a pad, shut the window, and got into one of the lifts.

"Let's see what's in that room," Joe whispered.

They slid open the window.

"It's puppies," Joe said. "Hundreds of them."

They peered in at the sleeping puppies. They were all identical.

Then one of the puppies opened its eyes. It began barking. The others began barking too. The noise was incredible.

"We'd better get out of here," Joe said. But suddenly, a security guard and his dog burst out of one of the lifts.

"Hurry!" Joe said as they ran for the bunker.

They hurtled down the ladder, one by one.

In the darkness, Joe heard a yell. It sounded like Roy.

Chapter 7 - The Patient

They stood panting outside the bunker lid.

"Where's Roy?" Joe said.

"He was behind me," Doug said.

"OK, let's think. Maybe he is hiding," Joe said. " I say we wait a bit. Then we go back in and rescue him."

"If they got him, they'll take him to the police," Asif said. He nodded at the sign on the gate.

"We'll keep a watch on the gates," Joe said. "Then we'll know."

It was getting late. There was still no sign of Roy.

Nothing had come in or out of the gates.

"I think we should go back in," Joe said at last. "He might be locked up or something."

The others looked scared.

"What's the worst they can do to us?" Joe said. "We can say we found the bunker by chance. Didn't know it was out of bounds."

Joe was the first into the bunker. But it was Asif who spotted the blood. A red trail led along the corridor.

"He must have fallen and hurt himself," Joe said. The trail led them to a room at the end of the corridor. Silently, Joe opened the door.

The gang stood amazed. Roy was lying on a bed, propped up by cushions. He was eating ice-cream and watching television.

His head and leg were bandaged.

"Hi, gang!" he grinned.

"What happened to you?" Joe asked, with a glance at the door behind him.

"I fell down the ladder and knocked my head," Roy said. "I must have cut my leg too. It really hurts. I just woke up here."

"Who gave you the food?"

"Don't know. It was just here. I'm watching the Simpsons."

"We've got to get you out of here," Joe growled. "Can you walk?"

"Think so."

Roy swung his legs out of bed. It hurt a bit but he was standing.

"OK, let's go."

Chapter 8 - Face to face

Roy's head soon healed. His leg took longer. Under the bandage, he had a long scar.

"Do you really remember nothing?" Joe asked.

Roy shook his head.

"You had a lucky escape. We all did." Joe said.

The Reactor really was out of bounds now. It was just too dangerous.

But Roy knew the people in there had looked after him. Perhaps if he got back in, just one more time, he could find out what was really going on...

So one night, Roy went back alone. He found the room where they had nursed him. A night light was on.

There was someone on the bed. It was a boy, about Roy's age. He had dark hair like Roy. He was sleeping.

Roy stood frozen in the doorway. He opened his mouth to scream... but nothing came out.

Then his clone opened its eyes and stared back at him.